I0701630

Death Gasp By Carter Pugh

Cover design by Donato Pizzuti

Edited by Melisa Graham

Published by Carter Pugh Writes LLC

ISBN: 9798988552093
ISBN: 9798988552062
ISBN: 9798988552025

DEATH GASP

A DEATH BOOK SERIES NOVELLA

BY CARTER PUGH

CARTER PUGH WRITES LLC

To death, may it grant us all the kindness not given to the characters in these books.

A death gasp is a brainstem reflex, the last respiratory pattern prior to terminal apnea. It is also known as agonal respiration, which is appropriately termed because the gasping respirations appear uncomfortable, causing concern that the patient is dyspneic and in agony.

Preface

Loud music blared through the speakers of my new bright-blue Jeep as Jenny and I sang horribly along with the radio. I'd had the time of my life at senior week, and its energy permeated the drive home. My new friend, Jenny Savini (whom I'd spent most of the week with because she was so much fun and a little wild), extended her cup towards me to cheers the roadie drinks she'd made us before we left Myrtle Beach. I felt like I'd gained a new lease on life. I'd had new experiences, I was about to be an adult and go to college, and I was going be free of my family and their rules and expectations. I felt a pang of guilt about spending so much time with Jenny and not my best friend, Amy, during the past week, but shrugged it off. She was a constant in my life and always would be; it was more than okay for me to make new friends.

The four of us, Amy, Kelly, Jenny, and I, had stayed in a condo together for senior week, and we'd had a blast together. Sadly, we were caravanning back home and back to reality. I was following Amy, and Kelly was riding with her. No doubt Jenny and I were having the most fun between the cars. I was slightly buzzed and was feeling giddy.

We were laughing, and a song came on that was too slow for the hype of our road trip. I often think that if I hadn't been drinking, if I hadn't been distracted, if I'd just let that stupid song play, maybe things would have been different. If I'd seen Amy's car had stopped at a stop light ...

But as it happened, I didn't even have time to think about putting on the brakes before my Jeep barreled into Amy's cream-colored sedan. She'd careened into the car in front of her, propelled by the force of my Jeep.

I remember a feeling of disbelief, Jenny's screams next to me, Amy's head hanging limply out of her car that bore no resemblance to a vehicle anymore, blue lights flashing, and sirens blaring, the first responder checking my best friend's pulse with a grim expression and a side to side shake of their head telling me everything I needed to know.

My best friend was dead, and I was the one who killed her.

Chapter 1

Heather

It was like that terrible scene in the movies—you know, the one when the protagonist has a bad feeling when her partner doesn't answer her call. She comes home early from work. She approaches the bedroom door that is slightly ajar, and she hears sounds that tell her precisely what is happening behind the door, but in that split second of time it takes for her to open it, she refuses to believe her instincts. Then she opens the door and is met with the image of a naked back covered in a glisten of sweat, grinding on top of her lover's body, and just as her mind registers that this is real, her lover calls out the other woman's name, shattering the protagonist's world.

It happened just like that, with all the grimy details. I was out a boyfriend and a place to live; I felt like I had lost everything.

I really should've seen it coming. My life had a pattern—blissful moments followed by heart-wrenching disappointment.

Granted, my childhood had been a golden one. I grew up in Winston-Salem, a smaller city in North Carolina. My parents owned a stream of successful dry-cleaning businesses. We lived in a three-story brick home with a large white wrap-around porch complete with a white-picketed fence. It was the American dream until I killed my best friend, and everything came crashing down around me.

Why did it have to be Amy who died? Amy, who wanted to be a marine biologist and save sea life. Amy, who had never so much as gotten a speeding ticket, let alone done anything wrong in her life. Amy, who had to work an after-school job to help her mom with the bills because her dad was a deadbeat who had abandoned them for a younger woman and a fancy new life. The rest of us in the accident had escaped with minor cuts and bruises. I may have banged my knee a little too hard on the crumpled dashboard, but I hadn't even let the emergency services look at it. I deserved the pain. It served as a constant reminder that I had survived while Amy hadn't.

The lawyers determined that Amy's death was vehicular manslaughter. I had been eighteen, stupid, and drunk on the feeling of the vitality of youth. And maybe, just slightly, drunk on some roadie drink that my new friend, Jenny, had made us before our drive home from senior week. It felt like the first naughty thing I'd ever done. Drinking some homemade wine or, honestly and more likely, moonshine out of a paper coffee cup. "Just in case we get pulled over," she'd said. "But officer, it's only coffee," she said mockingly as she giggled.

Since my parents were wealthy enough to hire the best lawyers in the state, I was never charged, and my record was expunged. The alcohol in my system was too minimal to impair my driving, they'd said. And they'd also argued that my breathalyzer test was faulty. I'd been much too numb to decipher the rest of the case when we were in court. My mom had slipped me some Vicodin to make sure I didn't do something embarrassing like cry or have some sort of outburst. I had welcomed the reprieve from feeling. Afterward, I'd taken to raiding her medicine and liquor cabinets to extend my vacation from emotions. I couldn't face what I'd done. The loss of my best friend would land too heavy, and I knew I wasn't equipped to deal with it. I was essentially still a child.

At eighteen, we're suddenly thrust from adolescence into adulthood and expected to know things no one has ever taught us and to be responsible in ways we were never prepared for. Especially me, since I'd had nannies, maids, cooks, and tutors my whole life. Someone to tell me when to study, when and what to eat, and someone who literally cleaned up all my messes. And even though my parents had saved me from jail time and having a felony or misdemeanor on my permanent record, they'd essentially cut me off from everything else. They'd saved me only to save themselves and their image. I'm sure if jail time for me could've been twisted in a way that made them look better, that's where I would've been.

I had six months to get a job, vacate their home, and remove myself from their sight. The shame I'd caused our prestigious family, and the family name, was too much. I felt like I'd lost my family as well as my best friend. Even before the accident, my parents had been mostly absent from my life. My dad worked long hours and traveled to business conventions often, and my mom's volunteering, committee meetings, and general society upkeeping made them gone most of the time. But this, this was a conscious effort to thrust me out of their perfect life. I didn't fit that mold anymore. Although, if I'm honest, I don't think I ever fit into the perfect daughter mold they'd thought I had before everything happened. My life had always felt too tight and suffocating, but it was all I knew.

Luckily, I'd be attending college in the fall anyway, making my lodging an easy task. They'd already paid for the first year in full, but it'd been made clear that I'd be solely responsible for the rest of the tuition.

College was going to be my saving grace; I'd be able to leave behind a town that hated me. The rumors of my potential drinking leading to the death of my best friend had eluded the main media but not the local paper, whose editor had a vendetta against the elite and privileged. I was cast as the villainous and careless murderer of an innocent and meek girl from the other side of the tracks. I was shunned by my own and hated by the rest. I welcomed the slander as I agreed with the articles. No one could hate me for what I'd done more than me.

At college, I hoped I could pretend to be someone else, anyone else. My drinking and pharmaceutical habits would blend in since, to most, college was the time to let loose and experiment. I could hide in plain sight, blend into the throngs of undergrads. I could lose myself, and maybe try to accept what had happened and move on finally.

I didn't deserve the life I had, but since the universe had spared me and taken my best friend instead, I was stuck here, pointlessly; I might as well get on with it.

A semester into my freshman year at Appalachian State University, I ran into a girl from my hometown, and the tale of what I'd done ran through the student body like wildfire.

There was no hiding the prying looks and constant stares as if no one in the school had ever made a mistake. Of course, the story had been perverted from a tipsy and careless mistake to a malicious act.

I decided to withdraw, transfer to another school, and legally change my name entirely. I needed to start over. It was extreme but fitting. My parents had basically disowned me, and our family name was too recognizable. I decided on UNC Charlotte to finish out my finance degree.

I became Heather Dunn and left behind the name that tied me to my family. I let Summer Simpson die that day in an attempt to start over and create a new life.

Along with changing my name, I dyed my light brown hair platinum blonde. I chose the tone because it was the color my hair had been when I was a child, a time in my life when I was happiest, and I thought if I looked like that again, those feelings would return to me.

After graduating and getting a job in Uptown Charlotte, I rented a small apartment about ten minutes outside the city center close to my favorite bar, the Flying Saucer. Going there and grabbing a few beers was an end-of-the-week ritual for me; it helped me blow off some steam and reset my mind for the weekend, which I lived for. I was content with my job. Correction: I liked the steady paycheck and the fact that I'd landed a job in my field directly out of college. I majored in finance and got a job at Bank of America as a financial planner for their upper-echelon clientele. It suited me since it was the world I came from, even though I'd left that life behind, having to work for everything I had since I was eighteen.

A few years later, I met the love of my life, Cody Mason.

Cody and I met at my favorite bar. At twenty-six, he was a couple of years older than me and was starting his career at his dad's law firm. He was on a fast track to taking over the family business.

We bonded over our shared love for beer and the fact that we both had a UFO plate on the wall. This was an achievement they handed out to patrons who had sampled two hundred beers in their establishment. My continued alcohol consumption was my way to get through and get on with my life after Amy died. Maybe someone stronger who went through the same thing would've sworn off drinking altogether, but not me. I didn't have that kind of strength. Regardless, I would have never met the love of my life if I didn't drink, so for me, it remained a constant companion.

I'll never forget the night when Cody walked into the bar. He was dressed in bootcut, dark-washed denim and a blue collared shirt, untucked. His dark-blond hair looked freshly washed, medium-length, and cut in layers. I felt like fate sent him directly to me that night. The bar was crowded, as it commonly was on a Friday night, and there was only one open seat right next to me.

When Cody sat down next to me that first night, he did so clumsily and almost knocked me off my seat.

"Whoa, there, little lady," he said, grabbing my arms before I fell backward and busted my head open.

He pulled me up and close to his body. Closer than he needed to, I noted. An embarrassing blush crossed my face as I blinked and stared at his deep-blue eyes.

"Hey, you okay? Did I ring your bell or somethin'?" he teased.

"Oh, no, sorry, you surprised me, is all," I answered. He was still sort of holding me to his chest and holding my wrists.

We both stared at one another for a second longer than was normal, and then Cody asked. "Can I get ya' a beer?"

"Oh, I still have one," I said, gesturing to my beer sitting in front of me, the condensation dripping down the ice-cold bottle. I took back my seat as he released his hold on me.

"Maybe the next one then," he said with a more than friendly grin.

As the night went on, we shared several beers and wigged out over the fact that not only were we both proud UFO plate recipients, but also they were right next to each other on the bar's wall. It felt like a sign from the universe.

"There is no way we haven't been in here together before. How I coulda missed seein' ya in here, I have no clue," Cody mused, his eyes dilating slightly as he inched closer to my seat. I'd let my feet dangle his way.

"I know! This is my favorite end-of-the-week spot."

"You're really beautiful; I love your hair," he said as he leaned in, almost whispering in my ear. His breath tickled and enticed me as he stroked my hair. I loved his easy way with me. The way he kept finding ways to touch me made me feel warm and not just from the alcohol. He hovered halfway back in his seat. Our lips were inches apart. His eyes flicked up and caught mine. I felt his hand cup my jaw as he applied gentle pressure, coaxing my lips closer to his. When our lips brushed, my body caught on fire. I was the most turned on that I'd ever been, and it was barely a kiss. He teased my lips with his tongue, and I opened for him. I tasted the combination of the beer we'd both consumed, and I wanted to devour him at that moment. While one hand stayed on my face, I felt the other snake around my waist. Cody pulled me closer to him, causing me to straddle him on his bar stool.

I loved the way his body was so much bigger than mine. I'd always been petite. I was five-foot-three and had a small frame and slight curves. He made me feel safe and warm as he surrounded me while we continued to make out in the bar. I was fully in his lap then, and all his deliciously hard parts were lined up perfectly with the softest parts of me. I tentatively ground into him, and he growled into my mouth. Things had escalated quickly, but we'd been drinking, and that had penetrated my normally shy exterior. And he was so sexy and sweet, and he smelled like cinnamon and a fresh shower. I was hooked like he was the sweetest sin; all I wanted to do was indulge. He was a deep pool of ecstasy, and I wanted to drown in him. He made me feel sexy, wanton, and powerful. Things that were not common for me to feel.

Somehow, we ended up in one of the bathrooms at the bar. When had he picked me up? I decided I didn't care as he started inching the zipper down on my work pants and then undoing the buttons on my dress shirt. I let my hands travel down his sculpted chest, dragging my sharp nails down until I hit the top of his jeans. Cody groaned as I struggled to unbuckle his belt and popped the button on his jeans. I heard the clink of the metal of his belt buckle as his pants hit the floor. I shoved my hand into his boxer shorts and grasped his hard length. I stroked him as he freed one of my nipples from my white lace bra. His lips left my mouth, and he leaned down to take the freed nipple into his mouth. He sucked and teased as a gasp escaped my lips. We rocked in tandem, eliciting moans and groans as pleasure shot through both our bodies.

"Condom?" I asked in a sultry whisper.

He looked at me with a cocky grin and bent down to reach into his jeans pocket. Tearing the foil packet with his mouth with a feral look in his eye, he handed the condom to me. I rolled it down his shaft as he made quick work of pushing my panties down my thighs.

There was no teasing with Cody. Which was great because I felt like if he wasn't inside me soon, I'd explode; I was drunk with need. He entered me with a thrust and covered my mouth with his hand to stifle the scream that left my lips. He pounded into me relentlessly as I wound my arms around his neck and legs around his waist. The slapping of our bodies was obscene, and I loved every minute of it. I'd never done anything like this before, and the knowledge that someone could walk in at any moment was such a rush that my heart felt like it'd beat out of my chest. When the walls of my sex began to clench, Cody bit down on my lip hard enough to draw blood. I felt his own release pulse as he came with a grunt. We broke apart sweaty, hearts pounding. We looked at each other with goofy grins and started laughing.

He looked like he'd been in a fight. I could see red marks forming from where I'd dug my nails into his neck, and there was a bit of blood on his mouth from where he'd bitten my lip. I'm sure I looked just as disheveled. I felt wild and free.

"I can't believe we just did that," I said through my laughter.

"I know. That was … you were … I really like you, Heather," Cody answered.

I winced slightly at the use of my new name. I almost wished that he could call me by my real name. But this was Heather's life, my new life, and maybe it was just starting to get good.

"I think I really like you too, Cody."

Before we attempted to leave the bathroom, we tried to conceal what we'd just done. Although, I'm sure we weren't the first to christen this bathroom.

I used a wet paper towel to wipe away the smears of mascara under my eyes and the remaining lipstick that was now all over the lower half of my face. My lips were swollen, and Cody had broken the skin a little. Like Cody, I also looked like I'd been in a fight. I loved it. Growing up, I'd adhered to a decorum of sorts. I was expected to be a lady, proper at all times. As Heather, I no longer had anyone to impress, and I loved the freedom it gave me.

Even if I never saw Cody again, the thrill of what we'd just done together would be a high I'd be riding for months to come.

Cody's arms swept around my narrow waist as he rested his head on mine. I looked up at our reflection in the bathroom mirror, and our gazes locked again.

"Wanna get out of here, beautiful?"

"Sure," I said with the first genuine smile and look of joy I'd had in ages.

Chapter 2

Heather

Despite my assumption that we'd only have one extremely sexy night together, Cody asked to see me again … and again after that. We were hot and heavy for months following that first night. Cody begged me to move in with him after a week, but I declined. He had a few roommates, and his home was a little messy for my taste. It looked exactly how you'd imagine a house with three guys in their late twenties would look—old pizza boxes scattered around, a full ashtray on the coffee table, abandoned beer bottles littering all the flat surfaces like confetti—you get the idea.

He wore me down after we'd been together for a year. My lease on my apartment ended, and I moved into his bedroom, putting my furniture in storage.

We were blissfully happy. We talked about buying a house while we built our life together. I couldn't wait to share my world with him. I wanted to have kids with him. For the first time since before the accident, I felt like maybe I could allow some joy into my life. I'd grown up a little since the accident and realized that even though some mistakes can never be taken back, maybe I still deserved a happy ending. Now I knew, of course, that I hadn't mean to kill my best friend. I had chosen to drive slightly impaired and had carelessly taken my eyes off the road briefly to change the radio station. Two choices made by a young girl who didn't know such small things could result in tragedy.

When we're young, we feel things so strongly; everything feels important. We're buzzing with life but haven't lived enough to know that not everything is as big a deal as we make it out to be. That somehow, the world keeps turning through heartbreak, death, and loss. Time moves, and the living move on with it.

Changing my name, dyeing my hair, and moving to a new school had helped me carry on. I'd pretended I was someone else until it felt real. In college, I was Heather Dunn, a normal college student who partied, woke up in random co-eds' beds, ate way too much pizza and junk food, and cursed early morning classes. I made memories and friends and graduated with honors. And now, I was Heather Dunn, a responsible financial planner and polished, loving girlfriend to Cody Mason.

True to their decision to write me out of their lives, I'd not heard from my parents since I'd left for college that fall. It'd been several years now, and I doubt they even knew I'd transferred schools or where I lived. When asked about my family, I'd normally tell people they were dead. For all intents and purposes, they were as dead to me as I was to them, so it felt true.

Even Cody thought they were dead. After dating him for two years and falling in love, I started feeling a deep-rooted guilt that he didn't know me fully. Some parts of me felt like it didn't matter; he fell in love with Heather, and that's who I was now. But another annoyingly and increasingly louder part of me kept nagging. How could he truly love me if he didn't know the entirety of who I was? I decided to tell him soon. I just had to work up the nerve first and think about how to approach it. Cody was obsessed with honesty and perfection, often telling me how much he loved me because I encompassed both of those things.

After a night of late-night drinking at our new favorite watering hole, Boardwalk Billy's, we decided to take a walk around the pond near the bar; it was one of those magical nights at the end of September when the air had finally cooled off, and the stars were bright. Even the ducks and swans in the pond seemed to be cozying up with their partners, enjoying the ambiance of the evening.

"Heather, thank you," Cody said as he slung his heavy arm around me. We were both a little sloppy drunk, and I stumbled a bit under his weight as I giggled.

"Thank me for what?" I questioned.

"You're just so perfect, and you're beautiful, and my parents love you. You were a hit at my company's Christmas party. You're just the whole package. You don't have any skeletons in your closet, but you still know how to have fun, and ya know when to button it up too. I love you, ya know?"

Ugh, I hated when Cody waxed poetic about how perfect I was. Sure, I'd adopted some new personality traits when I reinvented myself, but it still stung when he called me perfect. It was becoming increasingly clear that he was under a lot of pressure at work and from his family to live a certain life and be ready to take over his dad's company at some point. I understood more than anyone the weight of familiar expectations. I'd almost been crushed under the weight of them myself, but unlike Cody, I'd completely left that world behind. I was free from the constraints, from the vise of the decorum that comes with a prestigious name, yet I retained the memory of it like a brand on my soul.

I suppose that's why I was so good at interacting with his colleagues and family; they were "my people." But I had this fear that one day, the façade would crack. I'd make a mistake, a misstep, and everything I'd built would fall like a house of cards.

I realized Cody was staring glassy-eyed at me, waiting for my response.

"Baby, thank you, but no one's perfect," I drawled.

"You're perfect though," he slurred, leaning into my body further.

"I think you're pretty perfect yourself, Cody Mason," I said, turning into him and throwing my arms around his neck. He wavered a little since we were both unsteady but dipped down to suck my bottom lip into his mouth, applying small pressure with his teeth. Cody loved using his teeth to elicit pleasure. It was one of his kinks and one I immensely enjoyed.

We kissed under the stars. I felt like it was one of those nights when your life was on a high. I was in love and so happy.

"Let's go home," Cody suggested with heat in his eyes.

"You sure you don't want to walk around, sober up a bit more?"

"Nah, babe, you're good right? Let's go."

I panicked. I'd been careful not to drive after drinking since Amy. But Cody didn't know about that. The memory hit me so hard that I felt fully sober at that point.

Cody led me in the direction of where we'd parked his car. I had felt a little buzzed before the panic set in, and now I felt clear enough, and our apartment wasn't far. I had to shake off this feeling and get my head on straight. I was just overacting.

I couldn't stop the slight tremor of my hands as I got into the driver's side of Cody's Mitsubishi Eclipse. He was super proud of it and had upfitted it with LED lights on the bottom that illuminated the dark purple hew of the car. I backed out of the parking space slowly, trying to be safe, and almost backed into a car speeding through the parking lot.

"Heather, fuck, watch where you're goin', baby," Cody cooed, but his charming drawl didn't mask his annoyed undertone.

"Sorry, honey, they just came out of nowhere."

He placed his hand on my upper thigh, and my nerves calmed slightly. I hoped he was too drunk to realize how rattled I was. I shouldn't be doing this. I knew that.

Instead of voicing my concerns, I continued to drive us out of the parking lot, pulling onto Harris Blvd., which would take us home.

When we were almost to our apartment, the car in front of me suddenly slammed on brakes, and I had just enough time to slam on mine. Cody was thrown forward in his seat and then started yelling at me. An image of Amy's head hanging limply out of her car window flashed in my mind as the air evaporated from my lungs. I tried to breathe in but was met with a harsh resistance. I started to sweat and realized Cody was screaming at me.

"Heather, what the fuck?! Drive! First, you almost crashed into the car in front of us, and now we are just sitting ducks. I swear if the cops …"

I realized I was holding my breath and tried to start breathing normally without success. I started driving, not able to speak or respond to Cody yet. I felt a wet drop drag down my face and realized I was crying. Cody was still yelling his frustrations at me, but my throat was constricting with the grief of memory and the devastation over the way Cody was acting. He was drunk and didn't know why I had reacted the way I had. He shouldn't have asked me to drive; we should've walked around more, maybe Ubered home.

When I could finally speak, I apologized profusely to Cody. I felt like I'd betrayed a little part of myself because I knew that there wasn't a good reason for him to treat me the way he just had. I'd never seen him act that way before. He was always so loving, but at one moment of weakness … I was just shocked at his behavior. I knew, though, that it had to be something he drank. Sure, we'd taken the drinking a bit too far before, but maybe he'd had something that didn't agree with him. Maybe almost getting into a car accident had scared him too? Fear did fucked-up things to people, and everyone reacted differently. Both of our emotions were running high from the alcohol and the adrenaline from the almost crash.

I decided to forgive him—not that he'd asked for my forgiveness. He still thought I'd been in the wrong, and maybe to him, I was. He didn't know the truth, and maybe if he did, he would understand why I'd reacted the way I had.

I had to tell him. If we were to grow and move forward, he had to know. We loved each other, and I knew we could get through anything.

Chapter 3

Heather

One evening, I had finally gotten up the courage to tell him the truth. I wanted one person to know who I really was. With him not knowing, I felt like I was living a half-life. I didn't like keeping something from him. He could be so loving and understanding; I felt like I could trust him with this. I just hoped he wouldn't feel betrayed. I knew he had this idea of who I was—perfect, honest, without reproach. He often said how much he loved those qualities about me. It wasn't like I wasn't some of those things, but I had lied by omission, and I did have one really bad stain on my old reputation. But he loved me; he would understand, right?

Anxiety buzzed in my veins as I glanced at the digital clock on the oven for the hundredth time. Cody was due home any second, and I was both scared and excited to tell him the truth. I just hoped he'd be back before our roommates came home. I had no idea how long I had to tell him what I needed to, but I knew I didn't want to be interrupted. I was pacing between our living room and kitchen, likely wearing a path through the dust on our hardwood floors. As much as I tried, it was hard to keep our place clean while living with three guys. It seemed like they hadn't grown out of having their mothers do everything for them.

The sound of the door unlocking and opening sent my heart rate through the roof. I ran to the kitchen and took a seat on one of our barstools. This gave me the perfect vantage point to be front and center as soon as he opened the door.

Cody walked into the kitchen, where I was sitting on a bar stool facing him. His keys clanged in the catch-all dish, and he looked up.

"Oh, hey, babe, what are you doing sitting there?"

"Hi," I squeaked, definitely more high-pitched than normal. He seemed not to notice as he opened the refrigerator door and grabbed a cold beer. He popped open the top with our brass mustache bottle opener that read "mustache rides" and took a seat beside me at the kitchen bar. The bar stool creaked as if it was as nervous as I was.

"So what's up?" Cody asked, gesturing to the ripped-up napkin I'd been playing with.

"Oh, I didn't even notice I'd done that," I said, slightly embarrassed. "I wanted to talk to you, um, tell you something important."

I peered at Cody nervously. The color had drained out of his face, and his expression was ashen.

"Oh, no, no, nothing, bad, exactly."

"Whew, Heather, I don't know, babe. I thought you were trying to dump me or tell me you were pregnant. A baby wouldn't be the worst thing in the world, but we'd need to get married; you know how my parents are," Cody said, blowing out an exasperated breath.

"I'm sorry, no, nothing like that."

"Okay, well, what's so serious then?"

"I'll start at the beginning." I proceeded to tell Cody the whole story of who I was. It came out easily, considering I hadn't talked about this to another person in almost a decade. When I finished, Cody was quiet. He had finished his first beer and was already halfway through his second.

"Sorry, I didn't mean just to blurt all of that out, but I was worried the guys would be home soon, and I wanted to have enough time to tell you."

"Oh, yeah, they're both out of town on work trips."

"Oh, okay. Well—"

"So your real name is Summer?"

"That's what you want to ask me after all that?"

"Well, no, not everything; it's a lot to take in. Do you still want me to call you Heather?"

"Yes, Cody, I mean, I legally changed it. I wanted to leave that life behind and move on. I only told you because I love you and didn't want any secrets between us. Nothing needs to change except now you know everything about me."

"Okay. Sure. Yeah, that makes sense. Okay, so we're good then?"

"Of course, better than good. I feel such a weight off of my chest."

"Well, good, that's good. Hey, babe, um, the beer actually hit me a little funny, and I'm not feeling so hot. I'm really tired. I think I'm going to hit the hay."

"But you just got home. Did you not want dinner?"

"Nah, my stomach is a little queasy, and I caught a late lunch with some guys from work."

"Oh, okay, you sure you're okay?"

"Yeah, I'm just going to go crash." He turned, walked to our bedroom, and shut the door behind him, effectively dismissing me.

I watched Cody walk away, confused and wondering what happened. I knew I'd dumped a lot of information on him, but still. Was he trying to get away from me? Maybe he really wasn't feeling well. Maybe he just needed a moment alone. With our other two roommates out of town for work, I grabbed a blanket and pillow from the hall closet and made up the couch to sleep on. I didn't want to disturb him if he needed time alone. Whatever had altered Cody's mood, I'd allow him some time to digest either his upset stomach or his feelings about what I'd told him. Only about ten feet were separating us, but it felt like an ocean was between us.

I woke up to my alarm the next day and spotted a note from Cody on the kitchen counter. "Hey, babe, you were sleeping when I left; I had to get to the office early; see you tonight."

Huh? A weird uneasiness settled in my stomach. Something was off. Cody never went to work early. I guess it was possible that he had a meeting. I wracked my brain, trying to remember everything I'd told him and what could have him acting this way. He didn't seem to be upset that I lied to him. He'd not said that.

I wished Cody would have just talked to me. He'd shut down completely after I'd opened up and was vulnerable with him.

The other explanation could be that he was really not feeling well last night and really did have an early meeting this morning.

Three nights passed with surface-level conversations. Nothing seemed to be so far off that I could confirm anything had changed between us, but somehow, I knew it had. Cody avoided looking me in the eye, and when we made love, it left me so empty that I'd turned over and quietly cried myself to sleep.

My heart was breaking, and I wasn't even sure if there was cause for it. One thing I knew with heartbreaking clarity: the person I loved most in this world had shut me out. A small voice told me this was what I truly deserved: to have the promise of a life and then have it ripped away, to be punished with the same thing I'd done to Amy. The dark thoughts of Summer permeated my dreams and twisted my reality.

Chapter 4

Cody

The warmth of the whiskey hit the back of my throat and burned, easing the tension and anger that had been building since Heather, or *Summer*, whatever the fuck her name was, dumped her crazy past on me. Didn't she realize I was stressed enough at work? And what if anyone ever found out? I'd be part of it as much as her. She was her town's black stain, and I couldn't afford for her to become a stain on my life.

Another whiskey appeared in front of me, and I quickly downed that one too. For some stupid reason, I kept seeing images of Heather looming over me with a bloody knife. I mean, she accidentally killed her best friend in a car accident—she didn't murder her—but the notion wouldn't go away.

She'd lied to me about everything. I'd loved her. She was hot, perfect, and—shit, I'd even considered marrying the girl, was even looking at rings. What the fuck was I supposed to do now? I'd already put a deposit down on an apartment Uptown for the two of us, no more roommates. I was doing well at work, but with a decent portion of my money shored up in investments, I wasn't sure if I could afford the apartment without Heather paying for half. Damn it.

The worst part was it's not like I could talk to anyone else about this. It was fucking embarrassing. She made me look like an idiot. And I sure as shit didn't want to talk to her. She spilled this on me like we were talking about the fucking weather.

I pulled my phone out and typed *Summer Simpson* and *car accident* into the search bar. I might as well prepare myself for whatever shitstorm could be coming my way. The top search result: "Eighteen-year-old Summer Simpson was accused of vehicular manslaughter in the death of Amy Maynard. The incident occurred when a drunken Summer barreled into Amy's car after partying at the beach for a week. Summer is a menace to this town, and the fact that she saw no jail time is abhorrent. A sweet and innocent member of our community is dead, and Summer was the culprit. …"

I threw my phone down. Shit, I didn't want to read anymore. She was a monster and a liar, and she was hated by an entire town.

I sighed in relief as I saw a sexy-ass waitress arriving with my third whiskey. I'd not so much as looked at another girl since that first night with Heather, but now, I didn't give a fuck. Looking at other women felt like my way of punishing her for messing up everything. I'd never act on it … probably … but damn it, I was looking, and I was going to keep looking. Maybe I'd finally give in to the advances of my dad's business partner's daughter. She was hot as hell even if she talked too much, but maybe she'd shut up if I shoved something in her mouth. She had suggested more than once that she'd be up for something like that, but I'd turned her down, telling her I had a girlfriend. Fucking dumbass.

Who the fuck was I even being loyal to? I wasn't sure how else to process the fact that I had no idea who the fuck my girlfriend was. And fuck it, I still loved her lying ass or maybe just her ass. Well, I loved Heather, the version of her I knew—sexy as hell, perfect, obedient, fun, hardworking. Did I mention sexy? But this *Summer*, this girl who drove drunk and killed her friend with her car, if anyone found out, it could ruin my reputation. I was dating a national pariah. How would that look to the higher-ups at work? Shit, what would my parents think? They'd want me to dump her for sure. My competence could be called into question.

What a selfish bitch. How could she keep all this from me?

I downed my whiskey again and signaled for another one. I sure as shit was not going to deal with this sober; that was for fucking sure.

Curiosity won over, and I picked my phone back up and searched again, this time just *Summer Simpson.* Heather didn't have social media, but it looked like her dead parents had.

"Fuck!" I said louder than I meant to as other people around the bar turned my way. Shit, Heather was already making me look bad.

I scrolled through dozens of pictures of her very *alive* and *very* wealthy parents, sans Heather. She'd told me her parents were dead. Another fucking lie. At least I could work with this one. She came from money. That angle could work. I'd have to convince her to mend whatever fences she'd clearly broken, but I could definitely work with rich parents. Even if my dad discovered the truth about Heather, he'd see the potential of uniting two families with self-made men at the helm. My dad had started his law firm from scratch with his best friend from law school, Charles Villareal. Together, they'd created a veritable empire I was going to take over once the old goat retired. Heather's dad owned a dry-cleaning empire in Winston-Salem, and his net worth was impressive.

She was still a fucking liar, but I could use that to my advantage. She'd feel so guilty that she would never defy me again or step out of line; I'd have the perfect, obedient wife I deserved at my side. I'd have full control. My dad would respect that. We could explain her name change easily enough; she started going by her middle name. Yeah, that'd work. Didn't matter that it wasn't her real middle name, but fuck it.

I was a fucking genius. I just solved a huge fucking problem, and now I could do whatever the fuck I wanted without caring about the consequences. Heather owed me now, and I was bound to get my due.

As my vision blurred and my stomach warmed, I downed my fourth whiskey. I eyed the sexy waitress and signaled her over.

Chapter 5

Heather

On the fourth day after sharing my past with Cody, I was getting ready for bed when I heard the front door open. I'd worried myself sick because Cody hadn't come home for dinner, and he hadn't returned my text messages asking him where he was.

When I rounded the corner into the hallway and the kitchen came into view, I saw Cody sprawled out on the floor on his back, legs up like a bug with one leaning on the cabinets. His arm was outstretched toward the fridge. As he heard my approach, he turned his head my way, and I let out a little gasp. His eyes were glassy and bloodshot, the color of his face was muted, and he seemed unable to focus on me.

"Cody?" I questioned.

"Oh, babe, hey, I dunno what happened. I was tryin'a get a beer and somehow ended up on the floor." He grinned sheepishly as he half-slurred his response. His Southern drawl had become thicker as it often did when he was inebriated. The voice that had once charmed me now chilled me as if I had ice in my veins.

Knowing that he probably wouldn't remember this interaction, I decided placation was the correct course of action. Any confrontation at this point would end in a drunken fight, which would only worsen things between us. His drinking had gotten a little out of hand lately, but I suspected I was the cause of his stress and need to escape, so I didn't know if I had the right to question him about it.

"Honey, let me help you up, and I'll get you something to drink, okay?" I leaned down and took some of his weight as he poorly maneuvered his body to an upright position. My nostrils flared as I inhaled stale beer and whiskey. I was struck with the memory of our first night together. He had smelled like this, except it had been complemented by his fresh shower smell—it had enticed me. His current state repulsed me. The contrasting feelings collided, and my mood plummeted. Still, I fixed my compliant mask in place and helped Cody all the way up. Now standing, he swayed a bit into my body, making me feel uneasy on my feet. He leaned in further and smelled my hair.

"Hmm … you smell good, baby. I missed you." He was trying to come on to me, but all he'd accomplished was pissing me off. I really didn't want him to touch me like this right now. He needed to sleep it off, and I needed to convince him to.

"Thanks, honey. Let me get you to our room. It's late, and I'm tired; I'm sure you are after your long day. Let's get some rest, okay?"

"Okay, sure, fine," he said and pushed me forcefully away from him. I felt pain in my side as I stumbled into the corner of the kitchen island.

"What the—?"

"You're turnin' me down? Fuck you, bitch," he sputtered angrily.

"Cody, did you just push me, and what did you just say?"

"You"—*hiccup*—"heard me, bitch."

"Cody—" a sob broke through my response, and my throat felt too full to speak.

"I did some googlin'."

"What?"

"I googled you, *Summer*, about that accident. Your parents are *alive*. You're such a fuckin' liar. And you killed that girl—"

"Cody, seriously—"

"I loved you, and you lied to me, and I can't trust you. What am I s'posed to do? Sleep next to a killer? You act all sweet and innocent, but you used me. What—did you think I was too stupid to see through your shit?"

"Cody, stop, you—you don't know what you're saying, honey. You know me. I didn't—you know I didn't—you know I'm not capable. It was an accident. Cody, I love you. I'd never hurt you. You have to know that."

He looked at me for a moment. His eyes blinked, and he shook his head, the haze clearing from his eyes.

"Heather? Heather, what's going on? Why are you cryin'?"

"Cody, honey, we were … we were just arguing, and you … you don't remember what we were talking about?"

"No, no, I … I drank too much with the guys from work at the happy hour. I … I don't remember gettin' home. Are you alright? I'm sorry. Did I—I don't remember, baby. I'm sorry."

"It's okay, really. Are you okay?"

He rubbed his head and looked at me sincerely, "I'm sorry. I'm such a mess lately. I've just been stressed, and I think we did some shots, and I can't remember anythin'."

I stepped to him, and he steadied himself in my arms. "It's okay. Let's get you to bed so you can rest."

"Yeah, that sounds good, baby. Will you just let me hold you for a while?"

"Of course I will. Come on. Let's go to bed."

I know it's cliche, but he really wasn't like that when he was sober; he would have never done any of it had he known—had he been in the right state of mind. I began feeling like everyone's relationship must be like this. Everyone must have a dark cloud hanging over them.

That had to be it. No life was perfect, and mine certainly had never been. Cody and I were in love and had been in love for almost three years now. It was the best it would ever be, and I knew it. We just had this thing, and if I didn't say it out loud to anyone, if I kept pretending that I forgot what had happened that night, as he had, then the good time and good life we had been building didn't have to stop. The joy in my life, this beautiful treasure of a feeling, would stop spilling through my hands like sand. I knew it was my fault. I'd lied to him and shared my horrible past, and he couldn't handle it. I'd burst our bubble of happiness.

The next day, as I opened the door to our apartment after a long day at work, I heard music. The smell of garlic and warm bread filled my lungs as I saw the twinkling lights of hundreds of candles that seemed to decorate every surface. The apartment was the cleanest I'd ever seen it.

"Hey, baby," Cody mused as he took in my shock, my wide eyes and slack jaw.

I was speechless as I took the full glass of red wine he'd extended toward me. Clearing my throat, I tried to find the voice that had escaped me.

"Cody, wow, um, what is all this?"

He took a deep breath, and his charming face turned serious.

"Heather, I know I've been a mess. I know I came home a mess last night, and even though you tried to hide it, I know that I've hurt you with my behavior. And, baby, I am just so sorry, and I know that doesn't make up for treating you poorly, but tonight is just the start of me trying to make it up to you. I want to show you that our life can be what we have dreamed about. I want you to trust me and trust us, and I want to be that fresh start you wanted. I was being selfish and thinking about how hurt I was that you lied to me about who you were. I started thinking about what else you could be lying about, and I just lost it. I was thinking about how I could be perceived in all this if anyone found out who you really were, what my parents would say, and it just doesn't matter, baby. You're Heather, and I love you."

"Cody, I—" my voice cracked with emotion as he held up a hand to pause my interjection. I was filled with hope; he was saying everything I'd been longing to hear from him.

"Tonight isn't just about dinner and romance, although I hope there's some of that and then some," his smile turned rakish as he continued. "I'd like to ask you to move in with me."

"What do you mean? We already live together," I questioned, confused.

"I mean, I leased a new apartment for us—no more roommates. And I'm hoping I haven't messed up too much that you'll say no, and I'm hoping that you'll forgive me for leasing a new apartment without asking you. I'm sorry for that. I just wanted to surprise you. The new place is Uptown, so it'll be closer for both of our jobs."

My heart cracked and sealed back up in an instant. Everything was going to be okay. We were okay. I threw myself into Cody's arms and crushed my mouth to his.

Our need became fervent as shirts started flying across the room, and my pants ended up on the floor. I didn't even care if one of our roommates came into the kitchen at that moment. All I wanted was to be as close to Cody as possible. I had felt so close to losing him and had feared he would never touch me like this again.

Cody broke our kiss and leaned over to turn the oven off and burner to the warming setting. He turned back to me, smirking. His gaze raked down my body, heating my skin in the process.

I tucked my pinkies into the sides of my underwear and slowly dragged them down my legs. I stood back up and faced him. His eyes had grown molten. I reached back, unclasped my bra, and let my heavy breasts bounce out. I threw the bra at him, and he effortlessly caught it and threw it on the ground amidst the rest of our discarded clothing.

He approached me with purpose and spun me around forcefully, slamming my naked body into the cold counter. I heard his pants fall to the floor and then felt him lean into me. His cock was hard against my ass, and my vagina pulsed with need. I felt myself becoming wet for him as he pushed my body to lean over the counter. The coldness of the counter and the heat from his body sent my senses into overdrive. I felt a bite to my ear lobe, and I let out a sort of squeal-moan right before I felt him line himself up with my entrance. He entered me painfully slow, inch by inch. I loved fucking him this way. I loved the fullness; it overwhelmed me in the best way. Cody started pounding into me, my body continually slamming into the kitchen counter and cabinets. I grabbed onto one of the top cabinet handles as I held on while he fucked me relentlessly. I was screaming by the time he grunted his own release. We stayed there for a few moments, soaking in the aftershocks as the evidence of our mutual releases slowly ran down my thigh. I felt warm, loved, and safe as Cody wrapped his arms around me and guided me into our bedroom.

We made love two more times before we lazily ate the dinner Cody made for us in bed. When we finally fell asleep, we were completely spent and sated in each other's arms.

Chapter 6

Heather

It turned out that Cody coming home drunk and pushing me wasn't a one-time thing. After his apology and grand gesture of finally getting our place and moving out of his glorified bachelor pad that we'd shared with his friends, I thought we'd taken a step forward. I thought we'd be leaving the past behind and starting anew. Much like every time I'd attempted to do this before in my life, the past always came back to haunt me. Its ghost was a lingering pestilence on what should and could have been a happy life.

Our happy bubble burst three weeks after we'd settled into our new apartment. Cody came home around eleven at night smelling of whiskey and perfume that definitely wasn't mine.

"Hey, baby," he drawled with a goofy grin on his face. His eyes had that glaze to them he often got after overindulging, paired with red-tinged cheeks.

"Hi," I responded, my tone clipped.

"What's the matter, baby," he said, coming up behind me and wrapping his arms around my waist. His breath was hot and smelled of the alcohol he'd consumed. My stomach twisted.

"You were out late … again," I accused.

"Fuck, Heather, ever since we moved into this place, you've turned into such a frigid bitch." He chortled as he spun me around and leaned further into my personal space. I tried pulling out of his grip, but he applied more pressure to where his hands held my forearms. I could imagine the bruises he was going to leave; my mind was already conjuring up an excuse as to where they came from.

"Cody, stop it. You're hurting me."

"*Cody, stop it. You're hurting me*," he mocked as he pushed off of me forcefully, the impact causing me to sway off balance and fall to the kitchen floor, my head hitting the corner of the bar in the process. I grasped my aching head and peered up at him, not able to hide the shock and hurt on my face.

Hot tears built behind my eyes and began to fall down my cheeks. But I refused to speak up. It'd only make him angrier, and I just wanted the night to be over.

"Fuck, stop your cryin', or I'll give ya somethin' to cry about. You're so fuckin' dramatic. I didn't push you; your clumsy ass fell."

Luckily, he stormed out of the kitchen toward our bedroom, murmuring something like "fucking lyin' bitch" as he walked away. I only let out the breath I was holding when I heard the sound of the shower turn on. I let the tears flow freely after that, quietly sobbing and rocking back and forth, still seated on the kitchen floor. I was comforted in knowing Cody would take his shower and then head to bed. In the morning, he wouldn't remember a thing, and I'd pretend that nothing happened.

I felt like I wanted to run away, flee the feeling and situation. I wanted to run and hide somewhere safe until the storm was over, but I couldn't because I was in the storm, and the storm was my life. In a flash, the person I wanted for my partner, wanted to build a life and a family with, wanted to share everything with, was a stranger to me, an unreachable stranger. I couldn't pull him back from where he was; I couldn't save him. I was angry, so angry. At him, at me, at this imperfect world that just couldn't let us be happy. The fabric of who I was felt like it was falling away and crumbling from my body, leaving me a hollow shell. I was becoming numb, and at the same time, I needed to have a mask of calmness so that Cody would also be calm. The contrast of his indifference and eruptive behavior had started to take a toll. Bone-deep exhaustion was settling in, and I needed this to end. As I consoled him the best I could, the part of me that had reclaimed life started to die again. I tucked all my hurt and brokenness back to be examined at a later date once the dust settled. When everything was okay again, then I'd be able to put the pieces of my heart back together. My conflicting emotions warred inside me until I regained composure, clicking my emotions off as easily as switching a button.

Sometimes he could make me so happy that I swear my skin could not contain the joy I felt. And sometimes, when things were especially bad, he either looked at me with disdain and disgust when he thought I wasn't looking or, worse, wouldn't look at me at all. All I wanted to do was disappear, to not exist at all in those moments. This pain couldn't be sustained for long, but I couldn't find it in myself to leave him. He was my whole life, and I truly had no one else. Friends that weren't surface level didn't work for me because I couldn't tell them the truth. I'd seen what it did to Cody, and while I didn't really think that it warranted his erratic behavior, everything declined once he knew the truth.

I'd built walls around my heart to protect myself when I'd adopted a new identity, but love had broken them down. When I was vulnerable and trusted Cody, that's when he would strike and strike true. He knew how to draw me in; I loved him so much that I wanted to believe him when he said he'd changed, when he'd promise things would be different. I still came alive when he kissed me, and my heart still sang when he touched me, but with each intimate touch, a pretzel of whirling emotions of love and hate blurred everything into chaos.

I started feeling like everything I did was wrong; everything upset him somehow, so I just stopped. I stopped getting my hair done, I barely ate, and I was close to losing my job, having taken so many sick days because it was sometimes physically painful to pry myself out of bed. Any friends I'd gained at work had all stopped talking to me as a result of either indifference or agitation. I was a shell of a person, but as soon as Cody came into the room, I lit up, hoping he'd piece me back together. More times than not, when he got home from work, he would walk past me without even a backward glance—that is, if he came home at all. I spent most of my time alone, waiting for him. I'd stopped crying months ago; my tears had all been spent. We went on like this for almost a year after we moved into our apartment. It felt like we were roommates instead of two people who supposedly loved each other.

Chapter 7

Heather

After a surprisingly good day at work and a few unexpected flirty texts from Cody, I decided to get home early, shower, and make something special for him for dinner. He'd said he couldn't wait to get me alone and described what he'd do to me once he did. It'd been forever since he'd sent me messages like that—and come to think of it, forever since he'd touched me at all.

I rushed to the grocery store to get everything I needed to cook dinner and even popped into the Adam and Eve store to get something super sexy to wear after dinner for Cody. My spirits were at an all-time high as I bounded up the stairs to our apartment.

I swung the door open and headed straight to the kitchen, depositing all my bags on the counter. That's when I heard it—a creaking sound coming from down the hall. It was two o'clock on a Thursday afternoon. Cody worked until six most nights. No one should be here. Fear spiked, and my heart started beating rapidly. Was someone here? I grabbed a large knife from our butcher block and tiptoed toward the sound. I could hear heavy breathing as I approached our bedroom door. I raised the knife and slowly opened the door with my other hand.

At first, my eyes blurred, and I couldn't quite interpret what I saw.

My eyes trailed up the naked back of a woman astride an equally naked Cody. From the back, it almost looked like I was experiencing a memory of our past, like I was having an out-of-body experience. The woman looked exactly like me from behind. Well, what I looked like before I stopped getting my hair done and started losing weight. She was fit, blond, and—fuck, this could not be happening!

"Alison …," Cody moaned.

My wildly beating heart shattered.

I used to think that if anything like that were ever to happen to me, I would react entirely differently than I actually was in that moment. I thought I'd snap, see red, blackout, and then I'd scream and rage and cry hysterically.

That was not what I did. Without making a sound, I slowly backed out of the room and slowly closed the door. I turned around, grabbed my purse and work bag, glanced around our apartment, and made the snap decision to leave everything. All my essentials were in my purse and work bag, and we'd never unpacked my storage unit, so I still had all my furniture from my old apartment. Sure, I'd be leaving behind some clothes and toiletries, but those could be replaced.

Leaving the groceries on the kitchen counter, I walked out of our apartment and out of our life. I was done. After all the heartbreak, even all the love and happy times, this was happening; Cody was basically fucking a carbon copy of me. The me before he realized who I really was. The me before hurt and heartbreak diminished my appearance. She was sexy and healthy, and she was fucking my boyfriend.

My steps were haphazard as I meandered through the city streets outside our apartment. I ended up at a CVS and impulsively bought a box of brown hair dye. My hair was a mix of brown and blond since I'd neglected my hair appointments in my apathetic lifestyle. I wanted to erase Heather, the Heather that was Cody's: the platinum hair he loved so much, played with, complemented. And he obviously had a type if he was fucking a woman in our bed who looked just like me.

After purchasing the dye, I circled back to the public restroom and locked the door. It smelled like off-brand Pine-Sol and urine. Following the directions on the box, I mixed up the ingredients and shook the bottle until it looked right to me. I then squirted it all over my head and worked it into each strand.

I leaned back against the wall and looked at myself in the mirror … and began laughing maniacally. Cody and I began in a public bathroom, and here I was, dyeing my hair in a symbolic attempt to erase everything I was when I was with him.

I thought back to the sexy texts he'd sent me earlier that had filled me with hope. It was painfully clear now that those texts had been intended for *Alison* … whoever the hell she was.

After twenty minutes, I dipped my head upside down and rinsed my hair in the bathroom sink. I rang it out and tipped my head back up. My mascara was running, my hair was dark and wet, and my skin was sallow. I was a wreck. I was essentially homeless and had no plan. I had to get my shit together. A thought popped into my head, and I exited the bathroom, wet hair dripping. I walked out of the CVS and headed toward the center of Uptown. After a few blocks, I turned right onto Tryon St. and spotted the beacon of light herself. The green mermaid of the Starbucks was illuminated, beckoning me toward my destination.

After purchasing a Venti Americano, I sat at an unoccupied table, pulled out my laptop, and powered it on. Ignoring the glances I was getting from the other patrons, I logged onto my Facebook and searched for a group that advertised local apartments for rent.

I saw a post that a friend of a friend had shared about a girl named Clarke needing a roommate. She lived nearby and had an extra room. This could be exactly what I was looking for, something available now and close to where I worked. I reached out immediately, sending her a direct message. Dots appeared shortly after. She sent me a list of costs and the address and asked if we could meet sooner than later. I sent her a message back to tell her I could meet her anytime. She said she could come to meet me after work in about an hour, so I suggested the Starbucks where I was. Along with the hair dye, I'd purchased some makeup wipes and a few makeup products at the CVS, so I went into the bathroom to freshen up. My hair had already started to dry, and I was lucky that I had stick-straight hair. By the time Clarke got there, I looked halfway decent.

After about an hour, a brunette with long, wavy hair walked into the Starbucks and turned toward me. She was average height, curvy, and beautiful. She flashed me a thousand-watt smile that made her bright green eyes sparkle with kindness.

I waved her over to my table and shifted nervously. Clarke was kind, greeting me with an awkward hug.

"Sorry, I'm a hugger," she said with a chuckle when she realized I'd frozen like a deer in headlights.

"That's okay. I'm Heather. It's nice to meet you."

"So nice to meet you, Heather. I'm Clarke Carpenter. Looks like you've beat me to the punch." She gestured to my coffee on the table I'd been occupying all day.

"Oh, yes, sorry, I ordered without you."

"No worries, I'll go grab a drink and be right back."

"Sounds good," I replied with a warm smile and took my seat at the small round table. I shuffled my belongings around and packed up my laptop so that Clarke would have room to put down her stuff, then folded my hands and waited.

"So let me give you a run-down of rent and everything."

Clarke started giving me all the specifics of what I'd be responsible for and when everything was due. It seemed like she was giving me a deal, only charging me a quarter of the rent and utilities. She explained that it was because her room was the biggest and my room would be much smaller. I didn't care if she was offering me a closet, but I didn't say that to her.

I honestly had never met anyone as magnetic as she was. Something about her drew me in and made me want to be close to her. It was so weird, but I felt like we had met before. She had this way of making you feel at home within the first few minutes of meeting her. I may have just lost everything I thought my life was going to be, but I couldn't help but be optimistic. This girl was going to be my roommate now. She was overjoyed that I'd be moving in. I was struck a bit speechless by her candor and the easy way she spoke to me. We made plans for me to move in later that week, and I contacted the storage facility and arranged to collect some things out of it so that I could move into Clarke's. Until then, I'd get a hotel room in the city, pig out on junk food, and take some sick days off from work. I was determined to move in with Clarke, shake the dust off, leave Cody behind, and regain my confidence at work.

Moving day came, and I pulled up to my new home. The exterior was a dark-beige, industrial-style brick building. It looked more like a retail or office building with glass doors and large glass fronts to all the spaces. I pulled out my phone to call Clarke and make sure I was in the right spot before unloading my boxes.

"Hey, Heather!" Clarke responded cheerfully.

"Hey, um, I just got here—I think—but it sort of looks like I'm at a storefront. Am I at the right place?"

The glass door swung open to one of the spaces, and Clarke walked out onto a small concrete stoop, leaned against the rod iron railing, and started waving at me. Her brown hair was piled up on top of her head in a messy bun, and she wore a black T-shirt with some band name I didn't recognize on it with black leggings, her feet bare.

"You are in the right spot; everyone thinks the same thing when they pull up here. It's a mixed-use building, some residential and some retail, but they all look the same."

"Ok, great, that makes sense; I'll start unloading then."

"Awesome! I'll throw my shoes on and come help."

I grabbed a box and followed Clarke through the living area and kitchen and down a hallway to the left toward my new bedroom. This place was amazing and smelled faintly of sage. The living area easily had twenty-five-foot ceilings with ornate art-deco-inspired chandeliers. The kitchen had deep-mahogany stained cabinets, black granite countertops, and stainless-steel appliances. All the floors were the same gray/green stained concrete.

"This place is seriously cool, Clarke. It feels like something you'd see in New York. I had no idea that Charlotte had anything like this."

"I know! I found it by chance and fell in love. It was priced pretty reasonably because it's only a two-bedroom, even if the loft room could double as a separate living space if you added a kitchen. It's nine hundred square feet of open space up there."

"Wow, like I said, seriously cool."

"And here's your room." She guided me inside an empty, good-sized, windowless room with a large closet.

"See why I didn't want to charge you half the rent? No windows. I think it's why the price was lower than you'd think too, because, yeah, this is one of the two bedrooms, but who wants to be stuck with the windowless one?"

"Oh, believe me, I don't mind at all; this is great, Clarke. Thank you so much!"

"No, thank you! I'm going back to school to finish my degree in education, so I had to cut my hours at my job. Having you here will be a big help."

"Where do you work?"

"Oh, I'm a nanny for a family that lives two streets over."

"Oh … that sounds fun?" I questioned. I wasn't much of a kid person.

"It is," she chuckled. "I love the kids, and the parents pay me decently, so it's the perfect gig for me. Where do you work? I guess I should've asked you before, huh? I didn't even think about it. I was just so excited you wanted to move in."

"Yeah, probably," I laughed. "I'm a product of the city, I suppose. I work at Bank of America in finance."

"Oh, wow, that sounds important. Maybe some of your finance know-how will rub off on me," she smiled. "Once you get settled, maybe we can grab a drink at Murph's. It's right up the street, so we could walk."

"Um, maybe, if I'm not too tired."

"Oh, yes, of course, just let me know. I'll head out and grab some more boxes."

Chapter 8

Heather

A few months after moving in with Clarke, she convinced me to walk with her to the bar up the street. I let her help me pick out a cute outfit and acquiesced to her fussing with my hair. Somehow, she got my thin, stick-straight hair to look voluminous and sexy with a beach wave that I swear had to be created with magic. I felt beautiful and stronger than I had since I'd walked out of my life with Cody.

Clarke looped her arm through mine as she started to skip up the hill to Murph's, our neighborhood bar. I laughed as I started skipping with her, my heart feeling light and happy. She had this way about her that made me feel at home. Not my home from growing up—that had been a cold prison void of real affection. No, Clarke's feeling of home was warm, full of life, and freely given love without expectations. I'd never met anyone like her, not from my privileged world or the small reprieve of happiness I'd found with Cody. The best thing was, I knew, without a doubt, that she had no idea of her effect on the people around her, how truly beautiful she was inside and out. She was close-lipped about her own past, and I never pried, not wanting to reveal my own either. It seemed that we were both on the path to rediscovery, leaving our pasts behind.

The bar was crowded, as it often was. They had great drinks and even better food, but that night, it was the music that stood out. They'd brought in a DJ, and the dance floor was packed. A quiver of nerves ran through me. I could not dance, well not the way they were dancing. I'd run the gamut with cotillions, learning the waltz, foxtrot, and other various dances that I'd been expected to know proficiently for galas and charity balls. But to move my body the way everyone else was at Murph's, I had no idea how to be that relaxed. To feel the beat of the music and move, not caring what anyone else thought of me, was a freedom that I wasn't accustomed to.

As if sensing my apprehension, Clarke said she'd go get us drinks at the bar.

"Grab me a rum and coke?" I asked.

"You got it; I'll be right back," she replied with a smile.

When she returned with our drinks, we downed our liquid courage. Clarke pulled us both to the dance floor as one of my favorite songs started playing. Clarke's eyes widened, and she and I screamed at the same time, "I love this song!" We laughed, sang, and twirled each other around the dance floor. The night continued with a repetition of drink, dance, repeat. A bittersweet memory of Amy and I surfaced of us singing Spice Girls songs at the top of our lungs, filming music videos as we immolated our favorite artists. Clarke made me feel close to my best friend that night, and the thankfulness I felt for her friendship shone through my eyes as we drank and danced the night away.

She became a great roommate, and we went out a few times after that. We settled into a comfortable friendship. She was gone a lot for work and school, and I stayed late at work most nights, so we didn't see each other often. I was still very guarded, and despite the fun we'd had that first night, I still wasn't in the mood for too much socializing. I knew I came across as unfriendly, but I couldn't help it. My heart was broken, and sometimes Clarke reminded me too much of Amy. I was also afraid to go out and accidentally run into Cody or our friend group. I wasn't ready to see them. Cody had been calling me nonstop since my "disappearance." I'd sent him a short message saying I was done, moving out, and he could feel free to donate all my things to Goodwill. I needed to block his number, but a sick part of me didn't want to cut that one final tie I had to him.

Chapter 9

Heather

One afternoon, Clarke came home with a new friend she'd met at a concert she'd begged me to go to with her. I came out of my room to say hey, like the excellent roommate and friend I aspired to be.

"Hey, Heather!" Clarke greeted me excitedly with a warm smile. "This is my friend, Alison." She gestured to the tall blond whose back was turned to me.

I froze. It couldn't be, could it? This couldn't be a coincidence … it was her. It was the way the light from the kitchen spilled over the side of her face as she turned around to greet me. Even though I'd not seen her face that day, I knew, without a doubt, that this was the girl I'd seen fucking Cody. Her hair, her body … shit! She was tall, and her face was so beautiful. My gut twisted, and I was suddenly nauseous.

Instead of returning Alison's greeting, I left her hanging as I excused myself, mumbling about being sick as I ran to the bathroom.

I heard a faint knock at the door, and Clarke asked if I was okay. I said that I was fine and that I probably had food poisoning. I stayed in the bathroom until I heard the front door close, alerting me to their exit. I felt like a coward but didn't know what else to do. I was not ready to confront the girl who was probably still fucking my boyfriend. My ex-boyfriend. After almost a year, Cody was my *very* ex-boyfriend now. I certainly wasn't ready to hang out with Alison. There was no way the truth of our mutual "acquaintance" wouldn't be discovered. It could drive a wedge between me and Clarke—maybe she wouldn't want me to live with her anymore. I was getting ahead of myself, but I was panicking.

Really, what were the odds? My new roommate was friends with that boyfriend fucker? I mean, there is a chance Alison didn't know, but still. I was going to have to avoid her like the plague. What if she was full-on dating Cody now? What if they were sharing our bed and apartment? Horror gripped me as I realized that there was a chance he could come over to the condo to hang out with Clarke. I couldn't see him again. I wasn't strong enough. I had just started rebuilding my life. Or at least I'd stopped crying myself to sleep every night. That was progress.

A few months went by, and I'd successfully avoided seeing Alison again and, mercifully, had not seen Cody either. Sadly, that meant I'd backed away from Clarke too. I felt like I had little choice about it. Sure, I could just tell her about Cody and me, but I didn't want to put her in the middle. She seemed to be so happy with her new friend, Alison, and I didn't want to ruin that for her.

Clarke had mentioned hanging out with Alison, her boyfriend, Cody, and their group of friends several times. It was a little more than weird that they used to be *our* friends, and the sting of hearing her describe Cody as Alison's boyfriend hurt just a little too much. Clarke seemed not to like him though, which weirdly comforted me. She even went as far as to say Cody had made some comments to her that had made her uncomfortable. It made me sick to my stomach, and I thought about being honest with her about him a time or two. But after my life had gone up in flames the last time I'd been vulnerable and honest, I thought better of it.

Chapter 10

Heather

One night, when I had just drifted off to sleep, I felt a hand cover my mouth. My eyes flew open, and then I realized I must be dreaming.

Alison loomed over me in a black hoodie. The darkness of the windowless room shadowed her beautiful face, but the glow of my alarm clock on the nightstand illuminated just enough of her features for me to know it was her. This was a weird dream or, more accurately, a nightmare. Why would my subconscious do this to me? Had I not suffered enough heartbreak?

Something shiny flickered in the corner of my eye right before I felt something impale my chest. The pain was acute and overwhelming, and then I felt nothing; shock had rendered my nervous system dormant. I started choking as blood and vomit soared up my esophagus. I realized simultaneously that I was not dreaming, Alison had just stabbed me in the chest, and I was bleeding everywhere. I tried to scream for help, but her hand was still covering my mouth, and even if it wasn't, I couldn't take a breath deep enough to try to speak. I was coughing and sputtering, drowning in my own body fluids.

I felt what I assumed was a knife of some sort shove deeper into my body. I didn't understand her intentions. Was she so jealous of Cody's ex-girlfriend that she had to kill off her perceived competition? How had she found out about me?

As I struggled to take my last breaths, broken and baffled, I was shocked at how relieved I was that my life was finally ending; the pain of my existence was finally over. The last thing I heard was the unmistakable sound of high heels clicking on our concrete floor as Alison exited my bedroom. Peace would greet me soon.

Before her shadow vanished through my doorway, she turned around and whispered, "I'm glad it was you."

What did that mean? I was struck, confused, but my time had run out, and I knew I'd leave this life never knowing what the hell she meant. In my last moments, the voice I'd lost when Cody had broken my heart failed me once more as it tangled in my ruined lungs, which were now full of blood. My last thought was of fear, not for myself—I was dying; the worst had happened already for me—but for Clarke, who didn't know her closest friend was a crazy psycho killer.

As the last thump of my heartbeat sputtered and stopped, I wished that somewhere, someone out there would help Clarke through what would likely be a tragic turn of events. Then I closed my eyes and welcomed oblivion.

I felt a warm, glowing light and a flood of relief—and then my eyes flew open as a feeling of dread took over. The darkness in my bedroom morphed and moved, forming itself into a tall creature hooded in black. I thought it must have been the grim reaper coming to ferry my soul to the afterlife.

A peculiar, cloudy red mist swirled around the figure as it approached my ruined body and reached out a talon-tipped hand toward my chest. So fast that I didn't see it move, its claws dove into my chest, and pain seared through me. I was vibrating with agony.

I hadn't imagined death could be this violent. Was this what it had been like for Amy? I'd imagined her at peace now, even though she'd been killed so young. It had comforted me in my darkest moments, thinking she was somewhere wonderful in the afterlife. Now, only ten years later, I was murdered by my ex-boyfriend's new girlfriend, and then tortured by the angel of death. What was the point? Had I really been so evil to deserve this cruelty? So many thoughts were running through my mind as the pain subsided, and I suddenly had a sense of lightness. I felt weightless and … just … light, as if my body was made up of air and wind. *What the hell?*

I peered down at my ruined body as my soul hovered above it. The reaper seized me in its talons and dragged me toward a warped section of wall that appeared in my room.

On the other side, I could see a room with shiny black flooring and built-in black shelves.

As my room fell away, I had the sensation of rapid motion, and then I was unbelievably cold. *How could I still feel?* Nothing made sense. A feeling of tightness engulfed me as I was thrust into a small space. I was in the dark room I'd seen on the other side of the warped wall. The cavernous room stretched to a height taller than Clarke's condo and was full of shelves with oddly shaped glass bottles sealed with dripping red wax. Some appeared empty, and others were filled with differently colored, glowing, and shimmering substances.

I realized that I, somehow, or my soul had been contained in one of those bottles. This couldn't be heaven, could it? My soul was definitely not at peace. I figured this had to be some version of limbo. Could the other bottles surrounding me be souls as well? Was this penance for my part in Amy's death? For my wasted life after that?

The grim reaper stepped into view and leaned down level with me. Its black eye peered at me, creepily distorted by the glass separating us. It reminded me of the mirrors at a carnival funhouse.

"Hello, Heather. I apologize for your untimely demise. It couldn't be helped. I needed you for collateral."

Since I couldn't speak, the reaper continued as its coal-like eyes flickered through the glass.

"I require some things from your roommate, and I needed to acquire a good bit of leverage. You are part of a bigger plan that has been in place before anything you know existed. If you behave, I'll restore your life to you. Your current state could be permanent or temporary. It's up to Clarke really. But she likes you. I think she'll cooperate. Until then, rest, ponder, suffer … to be honest, I don't care what you do, not that you can *do* much. I'll return soon to collect you and see if you'll be of use to me."

The figure moved away, and I remained bewildered. What was going on? What did any of this have to do with Clarke? She was just a nanny, for Pete's sake. What had she done to anger Death itself?

Time went on through a sea of deafening silence that warped my perception. All I had left were my thoughts, which reeled through the emptiness that had been my life and was now my afterlife. I wouldn't be spared even here. No peace awaited me. Death, destruction, and devastation were all my existence was ever going to yield.

A NOTE FROM CARTER

You asked for more spice, and you got it! You might hate Cody as much as I do and be super happy that he is dead but admit it, Heather and Cody's start was sexy! I loved writing Heather's story and getting to finally tell you all that it's not necessarily over. (Cue evil genius laugh). Thank you guys for enjoying this little snack of a novella. Hopefully, it will help tide you over until Book 2 is done. It's going to be a big one, so you may have to wait a little bit, not too long, though. Thank you for all the encouragement and love.

I know this one was a tough one, filled with abuse, alcoholism, depression, and anxiety. Hopefully, you came into this story knowing that Heather likely wouldn't have a happy ending at the conclusion of Death Gasp. However, I hope you fell in love with her as much as I did. From the beginning of this journey, I knew I would be sharing Heather's story. I foreshadowed her importance in Death Rattle. I think I've said this many times, but I've wanted to share characters that deal with real-life struggles and show the pain that life can sometimes bring. Without spoiling anything, my goal with this series is to show how suffering often leads to amazing things down the road. Often in my life, I've experienced times so painful that I found myself in disparaging moments similar to both Clarke and Heather. I can attest to great suffering yielding great joy, and I want to showcase this as this series continues. If you are living in one of those moments, don't give up. Be encouraged; it will get better.

Perhaps, Tolkien said best, as he often did, in *The Hobbit,* "It's like in the great stories. The ones that really mattered. Full of darkness and danger they were. And sometimes you didn't want to know the end… Because how could the world go back to the way it was when so much bad had happened? But in the end, it's only a passing thing…this shadow. Even darkness must pass. A new day will come."

Thank you for joining me on this journey. I appreciate every one of you.

ABOUT THE AUTHOR

Carter Pugh lives in North Carolina with her husband and her puppy son, Cheese. She loves reading fantasy, romance, and sci-fi.

Writing has been a love and passion for her most of her life, but she didn't start her writing career until 2023 when she published her debut novel, Death Rattle.

When she isn't reading or writing in her spare time, she loves watching British TV shows such as Escape to the Country and Absolutely Fabulous. Carter's family is from England, and she has always shared a deep love for the country and its culture as a result.

To learn more about Carter and to follow along for more details on future releases, please follow on Instagram (@carterpughwrites) or visit her website (carterpughwrites.com).